Theories:
ATLANTIS

ELECTRA DESPOSYNI

AuthorHouse™
1663 Liberty Drive
Bloomington, IN 47403
www.authorhouse.com
Phone: 833-262-8899

Because of the dynamic nature of the Internet, any web addresses or links contained in this book may have changed
since publication and may no longer be valid. The views expressed in this work are solely those of the author and do
not necessarily reflect the views of the publisher, and the publisher hereby disclaims any responsibility for them.

Any people depicted in stock imagery provided by Getty Images are models,
and such images are being used for illustrative purposes only.
Certain stock imagery © Getty Images.

This book is printed on acid-free paper.

ISBN: 978-1-6655-5578-4 (sc)
ISBN: 978-1-6655-5579-1 (e)

Print information available on the last page.

Published by AuthorHouse 03/23/2022

authorHOUSE®

CONTENTS

PREFACE

Many years ago there was a gorgeous island inhabited by great looking, intelligent people, and giants.

This land of wonder, was the awe of the world. Originally credited for their righteous laws, and the sophistication of civilization...

(God Speaking)

The bad Angels (Demons), having seen the women of the earth, and filled with temptation of wanting them; came down from Heaven, and turned themselves into humans. Some women had babies with the bad angels, creating Giants.

CHAPTER 1
EARLY ATLANTIS

Atlantis was more beautiful than anywhere in the world. There was an ochre colored volcano (Hill of Cleito) coming out of a violet sea on the center of the island with magnificent mountain ranges. The hillsides shone with veins of white, black, and red marble, and contained every kind of precious metal, including the highly prized iridescent *orichalc*.

The rolling pasturelands had great herds of tame cattle grazing, and were as sleek and green as the waves of the summer sea. It also had lush planes with every type of animal, including elephants.

Atlantis had luxuriant gardens of which the fruit was really good and in infinite abundance. The flowers were so richly scented they made the warm air intoxicating. Every leaf on every tree glistened as brilliantly an emerald, including the olive trees.

The (lavender) water in the streams was crystal clear and fragrant as clover.

The women were beautiful and the men were handsome. They were also vigorous and intelligent.

CHAPTER 2
THE SETTLEMENT OF ATLANTIS

When it came time for the world to be split between 3 sons, Atlantis fell to Poseidon. Mythology has it that Poseidon was looking over Atlantis and upon climbing the Hill of Cleito, saw the most beautiful woman (Cleito) he had ever saw, and instantly married her, producing several sons who became kings of Atlantis with Atlas. Of which Atlas was designated as the king in charge.

It is now time of the **Great Migrations** of the **Stone Age.** The Giants, (called Colossi or Titans by the Greeks) located to Atlantis, a newly found and inhabited mass of islands. Atlantis was so newly developed upon Atlas' arrival that it hadn't been named, or had any structure. Thus, the continent of Atlantis became named after him. And he structured Atlantis.

The (demonic) giants were already present upon Atlas' arrival. (Whom were mainly from Northwest Africa.) Atlas (grandson of Noah) settled down in Atlantis and had 10 sons, whom became kings of Atlantis upon adulthood. Led by Atlas, they formed themselves into a counsel to rule the nation for the benefit of its people. The kings ruled Atlantis wisely.

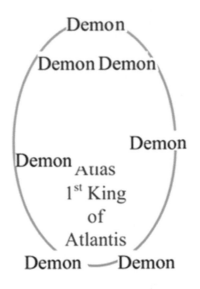

Demon

Demon Demon

Demon

Demon

Atlas

1st King

of

Atlantis

Demon —Demon

Demon Demon

Each one equally ruled 1/10th of the island, and their own tribe until the time had come to decide where they were going to live. The kings then split into areas.

According to Mythology the 10 Kings of Atlantis took the following areas:

1. Atlas- Atlantis
2. Ampher- Britons
3. Gadir- Spain
4. Evaemon- France
5. Autochthon- Germany
6. Mneseus- Burgundy
7. Elasippus- Italy, Sardinia, Malta
8. Azaes- America
9. Diaprepes- Scandinavia
10. Mestor- Mauretania in Africa

According to Biblical Figures the following were the progenitors of :

1. Ham?/Gomer?- Atlantis
2. Gomer & Javan (Sons of Japeth) Britons
3. Javan (Son of Japeth) Spaniards
4. Gomer (Son of Japeth) Francs (French)
5. Gomer (Son of Japeth) Germans by son Ashkenaz
6. Gomer (Son of Japeth) Francs
7. Javan (Son of Japeth) Italians
8. Ham- American Indians & Eskimo's
9. Gomer (Son of Japeth) Scandinavians
10. Shem or Ham- Mauretania, Africa (one of Hams' sons settled Egypt)

For approximately 3,000 years and several generations Atlanteans enjoyed the peace under a system of laws that had been handed down to them by their "God", whose justness was admirable.

The second king of Atlantis was supposedly Gaderios (brother to Atlas), and the kingship of Atlantis was passed down through the eldest son.

The capital of Atlantis was "Brasília" where the "King of the World" resided.

Their culture was called Megalithic.

Their religion was Sumerian Zeroashtaism (the worship of a God personified by the sun).

Poseidon was their "God," and father of the original Atlanteans. Cleito was the mother of the original Atlanteans.

On the center of the island, was the Hill of Cleito, where her sons had built her a great Imperial Palace. The Imperial Palace was made of red, white, and black marble and was blazed with inlays of gold and precious stones.

In the main city they had also built a temple to Poseidon.

The temple was the wonder of all the world. The Atlantean's (people of Atlantis) had built it so tall that the clouds swirled the tip of it. It was built of white, black, and red sandstone (marble) and covered with silver, the pinnacles were covered with gold. The ceiling was made of ivory, wrought with gold and silver. The pillars, walls, and floor were coated with orichalc. It was blazed with inlays of gold and precious stones.

Inside the temple of God (Poseidon), they placed statues of gold. They had built a statue of God (Poseidon/Neptune) riding on a chariot with six winged horses, surrounded by 100 Nereids/ Nymphs riding on dolphins. The statue was so tall, the charioteer hit the ceiling with his head. The Laws of God were inscribed on a pillar of orichalc inside the temple, by the first kings.

The Kings of Atlantis would meet at this temple. Shortly after building the temple they had met and made a pact to benefit the people of Atlantis. They would meet on a regular basis. Every 5 years they would have a festival during their legislative meeting in which stockmen would gather the finest bulls and corral them on the temple grounds. Once the meeting ended, the hunters would dodge the charges of the bulls until they could corner one and wrestle it to the ground. They would then sacrifice the bull to the glory of Poseidon.

CHAPTER 3
THE EVOLVEMENT OF ATLANTIS (HISTORICAL)

"Brasilia" demonstrated the high level of civilization achieved by the Atlanteans in ancient times. It was "marvelous beyond all description." (Plato)

They excelled in art and science. They invented reading, writing, math, agriculture, architecture, and all forms of civilization. The people of Atlantis were also very willing and generous to share all their knowledge with whomever they came in contact with. They shared their knowledge of metallurgy, astronomy, medicine, magnetism, etc. They taught the Mayans and Egyptians how to build pyramids, and the Greeks how to construct sculptures...

The city's buildings were large scale and were of dazzling, decorative splendor.

The city's main port or harbor was always bustling (busy). It was full of ships and merchants from all over, thus making Atlantis very wealthy and prosperous. They had developed a distinctive culture (megalithic) that became the mother culture to Egypt, Britain, and Mexico.

The circles of land and trenches around the Hill of Cleito were linked by great bridges. The city was further enhanced by gorgeous gardens, groves of flowering trees, and innumerable sparkling fountains.

During the **New Stone Age**, Atlanteans rose to great power. During this time they sent out explorers and began expanding by establishing colonies and outposts along the coasts of the Atlantic Ocean. During this time they had become the center of a trans-Atlantis maritime empire. They mined tin in Britain and copper in Ireland, which they took back to their smelteries in Atlantis to make bronze. The Atlanteans then exported the bronze to the British Isles starting Britain's **Bronze Age**.

During the **New Stone Age** (2.6 million years ago until 3300 BC), the Atlanteans were trading with the British Isles and England. (Greece began working with bronze by 3,000 BC). It's possible bronze was in use as early as 6,000 years ago...The British Isles started using bronze around 1900 BC during the bronze age.

Middle Stone Age By orders of Azaes, Atlantanteans started settling in North America by way of the British Isles in the Northern Arc. They settled along the Great Lakes (Azatalan) and moved down the Mississippi into Mexico. The people of Azatalan were known as "Mound-Builders" for building large earthen mounds that are believed to be the pro -type to pyramids. They were also the ancestors to the Aztecs and Chichimec tribes and were the successors of the great tribes/nations of Central America.

Also during this time, some colonists (to be known later in time as "PICTs") started settling in Britain.

By **Early Bronze Age** (before 3300 BC), the Atlanteans were trading with Italy, Libya, and Egypt.

Early Bronze Age during this time they had begun to expand into western Mediterranean waters: Libya, Egypt, Italy, and Isle of Malta. During this time Sumerian Zeroashtaism mixed with local culture and emerged as "Druidism" in Britain, Ireland, and then Gaul (France).

By the **Bronze Age**, the Atlantean's had been trading with Northwest Africa, North America, Western Europe, and Scandinavia.

During the **Middle Bronze Age**, Atlantis lost its hegemony over Western Europe.

Late Bronze Age The 3rd wave of Atlanteans came to the Americas as refugees from the destruction of Atlantis. They settled in the shores of the Gulf of Mexico, working their way up through New Mexico and Colorado becoming known as the Olmecs, Xicalancans, and Mayans. The "Mound- Builders" were their successors.

During an era of corruption, while the Atlantean kings had become greedy, they met for one of their gatherings and had decided to wage war on their trading/bartering partners (the world) as they felt they should be owed tribute for their generosity of sharing their cultural advancements with them. "This vast empire gathered all its forces together (allied with Britain), and undertook to conquer all the lands that border the Mediterranean Sea." (Plato) Thus, they started their conquest of the world.

One group set out to Central and South America, attacking the Incas, Aztecs, and Mayas, sending back their raided loot to Atlantis. With Britons as their allies, another force conquered all of North Africa before regrouping in Egypt to attack Greece and then Asia.

When the Atlanteans arrived in Athens, Greece, the Athenians were waiting for them. The Atlanteans destroyed the Minoan Empire of Crete, attacked Mycenaean Greece, and the 18th Dynasty Egypt. However, Athens, Greece was the only place that was able to withhold and defeat the Atlantean's siege, but the Greek Navy was destroyed in a storm, while in pursuit.

About **2700 BC** the Atlanteans had overran Greece, the Near East, and Egypt.

By **2600 BC** the Mesopotamians (Sumerians) had driven the Atlanteans out of the eastern Mediterranean region.

By **2100 BC** the Minoans had driven out most of the Atlanteans from the western Mediterranean region. These Atlanteans remained in the Near East (land of Canaan) and battled the Hebrew tribes. The ones driven out settled in the Caucasus, the Crimea, and in Bulgaria.

Upon later being driven out from there, they migrated to Syria, Northern Iran, the Malabar Coast, the Nilgiri Hills of India, to South- Eastern Asia, and then to the South Sea Islands. Where there is no history of them once the Polynesians settled the Pacific Islands.

After battling with the Mediterraneans, the Atlanteans of Atlantis withdrew into the Atlantic Ocean and ruled Supremely as isolationists for the next 500 years. The only interaction they had with the outside world was the piracy of Mediterranean ships that ventured past the Straights of Gibraltar. Those crew members were taken captive and used as slaves to work in the mines and smelteries. One of these enslaved captives was the Etruscan Italian King/Greek Prince, Corythus (Demetrius).

CHAPTER 4
DESTRUCTION

At the time of the destruction of Atlantis, (Approximately **1500 BC**), it had possessed a high level of civilization.

The people of Atlantis became corrupt. They were greedy and started to worship the false Gods of **wealth, idleness, and luxury,** during a time of corruption. At a time when they were again at war with the Mediterranean people, the destruction of Atlantis happened.

"In a single day and night of misfortune" (Plato) there was violent earthquakes and floods. In which Atlantis was destroyed by a "terrible convulsion of nature" (a horrific natural cataclysm) as the Atlantean fleet was about to set sail. A choking heat engulfed the island, the sky turned the color of dry blood, a mass of black clouds making a dreadful sound swept across the sky, the sea turned the color of lead, and rose in gigantic waves of up to 200′ which engulfed the island, and the Atlantean fleet. Atlantis sunk beneath the sea where only the tips of its mountains (Azore Islands?) show.

According to Plato, Atlantis disappeared with nearly all of its inhabitants beneath the Sea. Once the sea calmed down a few surviving battered ships crept into port, delivering the news that Atlantis had disappeared by the ocean rolling over it.

CHAPTER 5
ATLANTEANS TODAY

The Atlanteans that escaped the destruction went east settling in the Pyrenees Mountains between France and Spain (known as <u>Basque</u> people), north settling in the northern British Isles (Ulster, Ireland, & Northern Scotland), the Nordreys, (Orkney Islands, Shetland's, & Faroes) and the Trondheimfjord area in Western Norway (known as the Atecotti/ Attacotti people who later became part of the <u>Picts</u>), and west settling in Central America known as the <u>Olmecs</u> (ancestors to the Mayans).

Under the leadership of the Atlantean, Prince Creon (1st tribal chief/king of the Atecotti and ancestor to Britains 3rd royal dynasty, the Creons) the Atlanteans relocated northwards.

Cronos (III) (Crosus, Crocus) the last king of Atlantis, was survived by an only child. His daughter, Antyllia (Electra), who was saved by a group of ex-slaves, one of which was Corythus. Electra is believed to be the mother of Dardanius. She had married Corythus. Yet, there is debate whether Corythus or Zues (Zarah son of Judah) is the father as Zues lusted for her.

The Basque people still exist. A common maternal haplotype found among them is H3c, which is allegedly also the same maternal haplotype (H3) as Cerdic. (The founder of English Royalty.)

INTERFACE

To everyone who has read this:

I would like to thank you for taking the time to read my view on Atlantis. I hope you enjoyed it.

For further reading, please look for my next book, "Theories: European Royalty"

I hope you will enjoy the sequel, as well.

Thank you & God Bless

Printed in the United States
by Baker & Taylor Publisher Services